Reading Together

Beans on Toast

D1312261

Read it together

Baked beans, beans on hot dogs, and beans on toast! Here's a chance for children to see where beans come from in this enjoyable information book.

One of the most important ways of helping your child to read is by reading aloud, and this is true of information books too. It's a good way of introducing children to a wide variety of different kinds of books.

This is a new one!

I wonder where the beans will go next?

They'll go to the shop.

This book shows how baked beans are produced. Children can use the cartoon-style pictures to predict the next stage in the process and to match their ideas to the words on the page.

*Beans on a tray
Beans on the truck
Beans on the hill . . .*

With experience, and help from the pictures and the repeated word pattern, children may be reading this book for themselves quite quickly. Don't worry if the words aren't always the same as those on the page.

Beans on Toast

Paul Dowling

CANDLEWICK PRESS

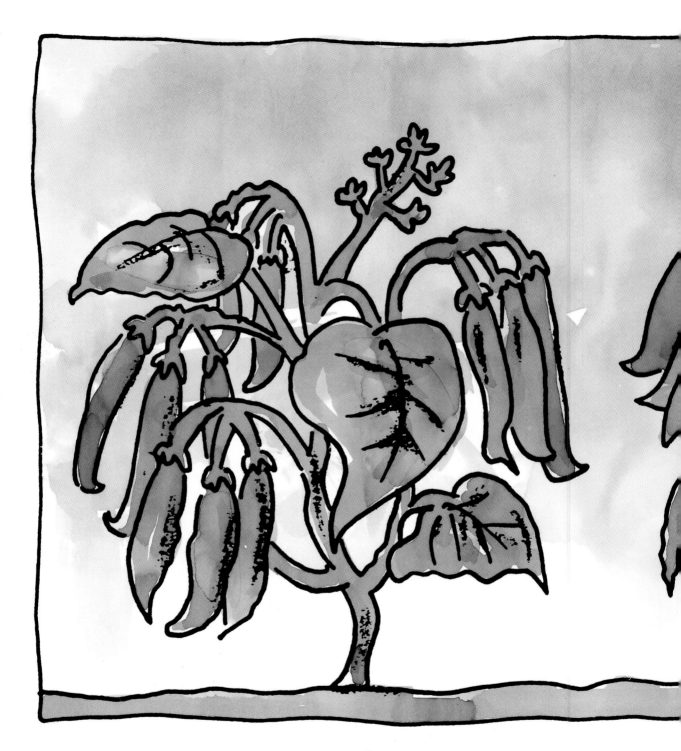

Beans on stalks.

If children are reading and get stuck on a word, you can help them guess. Encourage them to look at the pictures and the first letter of the word, or to read on and come back to it. It's a good idea to just tell them the word if they're really stuck or tired.

Sometimes you can help children to look more closely at the actual words and letters. See if they can find words they recognize, or letters from their name. Help them write some of the words they know.

Talk about books with them and discuss the stories and pictures. Compare other books with *Beans on Toast*.

We hope you enjoy reading this book together.

For Carol and Peter

Copyright © 1998 by Paul Dowling
Introductory and concluding notes copyright © 1998 by CLPE/L B Southwark

Second U.S. edition in this form 1999

Library of Congress Catalog Card Number 98-88066

ISBN 0-7636-0875-0

4 6 8 10 9 7 5

Printed in Hong Kong

Candlewick Press
2067 Massachusetts Avenue
Cambridge, Massachusetts 02140

Beans on legs.

Beans on racks.

Beans on wheels.

Beans on the road.

Beans on crane.

Beans on the boil.

Beans on cans.

Beans on trucks.

Beans on shelves.

Beans on counter.

Beans on the way home.

Beans on stove.

Beans on spoon.

Beans on head.

Beans on floor.

Beans on toast.

Read it again

Map the journey

This book shows, in an amusing way, how beans move from the field to the plate. With your help, children can map the journey in a simple diagram. Perhaps they can act it out, too.

Plan the day

Many everyday activities can be mapped out, such as cooking, painting, and getting dressed. You could plan one out together.

> First I put on my underwear, then my socks. . . .

What happens next?

You could talk together about what happens after the end of the story in the book. Your child can draw what happens to the bean can.

> Mom put the empty can in the trash . . .

> and then the garbageman took it to be recycled and made into a new can.

> And maybe we bought it again when we went shopping!

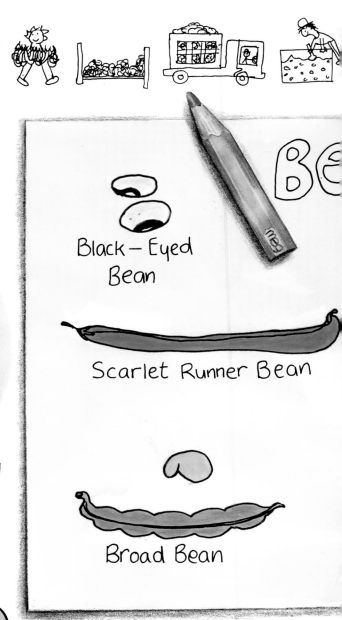

Black — Eyed Bean

Scarlet Runner Bean

Broad Bean

BE

Beans, beans, beans!

When shopping or cooking together, you can look at different kinds of beans — fresh and canned. Children can talk about them, taste them and draw them. They can describe them for you, and you can write a label next to each picture.

ns

Soybean

Red Kidney Bean

Lima Bean

aricot
ean

Baked beans are made with haricot beans.

I like lima beans best.

Speech bubbles

Go through the book with your child and imagine what the characters on each page might be saying or thinking.

The words can be written on cards, then cut out and placed on each page. Children might like to play a game of matching these bubbles to the pictures as they read through the book with you.

I'm the truck driver.

Beans on the road.

wheels

Bean recipe

Your child can help you make a favorite meal with beans. Afterward, with your help, they can draw and write it down as a recipe.

I like beans best with hot dogs.

Reading Together

The Reading Together series is divided into four levels—starting with red, then on to yellow, blue, and finally green. The six books in each level offer children varied experiences of reading. There are stories, poems, rhymes and songs, traditional tales, and information books to choose from.

Accompanying the series is the *Reading Together Parents' Handbook,* which looks at all the different ways children learn to read and explains how *your* help can really make a difference!